This edition published by Parragon Books Ltd in 2015

Parragon Books Ltd
Chartist House
15–17 Trim Street
Bath BA1 1HA, UK
www.parragon.com

Copyright © 2015 Disney Enterprises, Inc.

Based on an episode by Laurie Israel and Rachel Ruderman
Adapted by Catherine Hapka
Illustrated by Grace Lee

ISBN 978-1-4723-8998-5

Printed in China

Disney
Sofia
the First
Princesses to the Rescue!

Adapted by
Catherine Hapka

Based on an episode by
Laurie Israel and
Rachel Ruderman

Illustrated by
Grace Lee

PaRRagon

Bath • New York • Cologne • Melbourne • Delhi
Hong Kong • Shenzhen • Singapore • Amsterdam

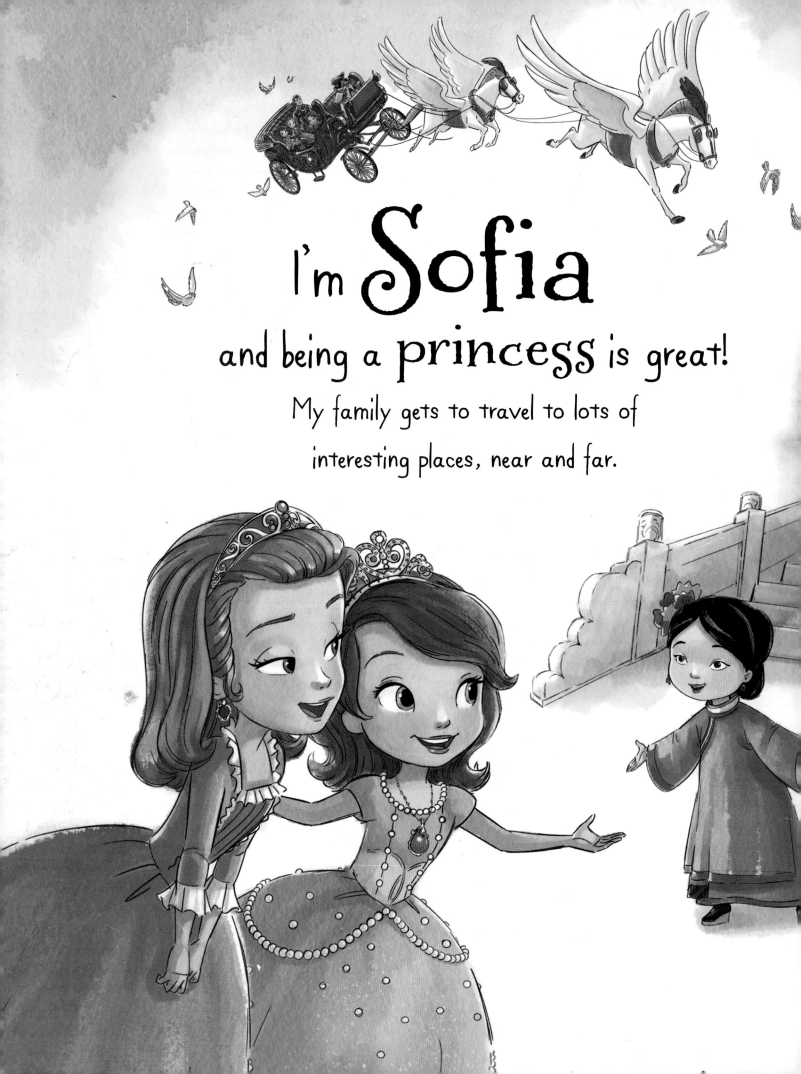

I'm Sofia
and being a princess is great!

My family gets to travel to lots of
interesting places, near and far.

Today we're visiting
the amazing **kingdom** of Wei-Ling.
Our friends Princess Jun and Prince Jin live here.

Soon after we arrive, James and Jin discover
a map to the **treasure** of the Jade Jaguar.
Before we know it, they're
running off to find it!

When we tell Jin's dad,
Emperor Quon,
where the boys went,
he looks worried.

"A **real** jaguar guards that treasure!" he exclaims. "We must stop them! Let's go!"

"We want to go with you and help," I say.

But the emperor says it's too dangerous for princesses. Then he and my dad rush off.

I'm very worried, especially when the royal **sorcerer** Wu-Chang tells us about the trap the jaguar set to protect his treasure. Our brothers and fathers could become trapped!

Wu-Chang explains how to find the jaguar's cave.
He even tells us about a secret entrance!
"I will send for the guards to help," he says.
"But you must leave now."

We set out on the path, but soon we see
some giant stone statues blocking our way.

Jun spots a sign that says
'The Maze of Warriors'.
We try to enter the maze ...
but a Stone warrior moves
over and blocks us!

"That statue moved!" Jun exclaims.

Amber nods. "Sofia, this is getting creepy."

"Let's try again," I say. But no matter which way we try to go, the statues block our path.

Amber and Jun are ready to give up.

"If we can't even make it past statues,

how are we going to get past a jaguar?" says Jun.

Maybe Amber and Jun are right.

Maybe we **should** turn back.

Then I notice my amulet.

It's **glowing!**

We turn round and
there's Mulan!
"Where do you think you're going?"
she asks us with a smile.
"I never gave up so easily.
And neither should you.
You girls are stronger
than you know."

Mulan helps me climb on to a statue.

I leap to the next statue and the one after that.

Amber and Jun see they can do it, too,

and before we know it ...

"We made it!" Amber cries.

"See?" Mulan says.

"You girls are stronger than you thought."

"But we still have to save our families," I remind her.

"Can you help us, Mulan?"

"You have what it takes to get past anything
that comes your way," Mulan says.
So we continue along the path, but when I look back,
Mulan is gone.

A little further down the path,
we hear a **buzzing** noise.
Suddenly, we're surrounded by moths.
There are so many that we can't
see where we're going!

"No way am I letting a bunch of
noisy bugs mess up my hair," Amber declares,
using her fan to shoo them away.

"Wow, Amber," I say. "That was **amazing!**" Amber twirls her fan. "Now I'm ready to face that jaguar," she says.

"I'm glad you're feeling braver, Amber," I say. "We need all the help we can get!"

Next the path leads to a lagoon
with huge scary-looking lizards
crouching on the shore.

"Lagoon lizards," Jun explains.
"The meanest lizards in all of Wei-Ling!"

Amber tries to shoo the nearest lizard away with her fan, but it takes a **big** bite out of it!

"I **just** remembered something," Jun says, grabbing her flute. "Music calms them down." She begins to play a song.

Like **magic**,
the Lagoon Lizards stop snapping
their jaws and sway to the music.
I crouch beside one and whisper,
"Mr Lizard, could you take us across the lagoon?"
"We'd be happy to as long as
she keeps making music,"
the lizard replies.

I call to Amber and Jun.

"Look! These lizards are heading across. Let's hop on!"

It works!

Jun keeps playing music and the lizards carry us safely across the lagoon.

On the other side, there's a **waterfall**.
Then I spot something behind the wall of water: the
secret entrance to the cave Wu-Chang told us about!

We crawl through the
narrow tunnel entrance into the cave.
"Look at all the jewels!"
Amber exclaims.

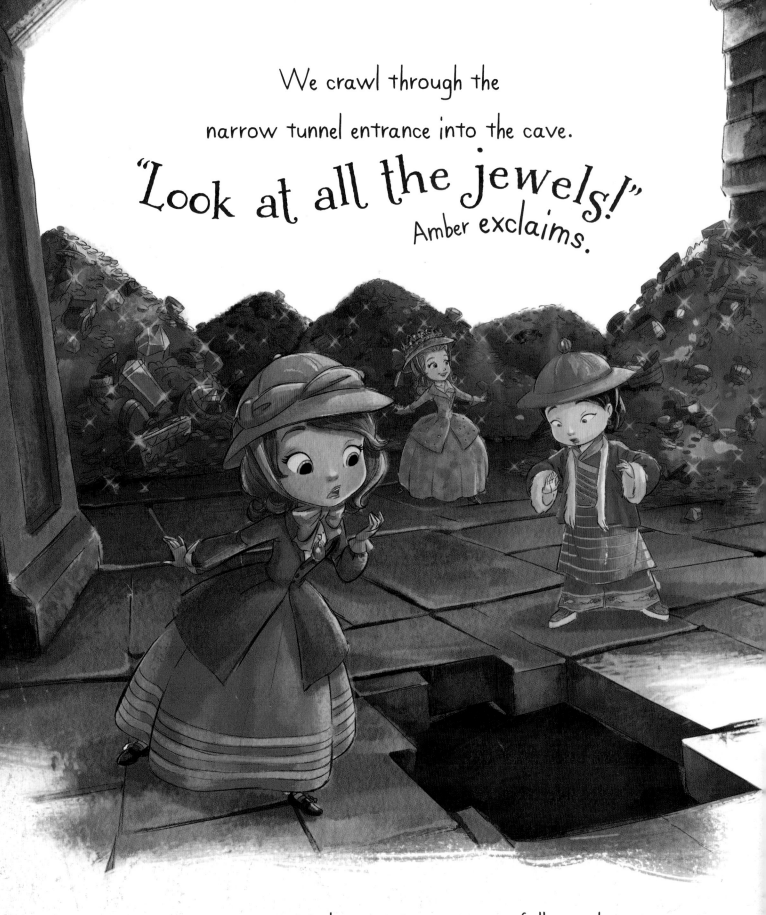

We hear voices, so we follow them,
and we find everyone trapped in a deep pit.

"James! Dad!" I cry.
Dad looks amazed.
"You girls shouldn't be here,"
he says.

Suddenly, the Jade Jaguar leaps out from behind his treasure!

ROAR!!!

Amber and Jun hide, but it's too late to turn back. We have to save our families. I have an idea! I grab a handful of jewels....

"You **want** these back?" I say to the jaguar. "**Then catch me!**"

I scramble back into the narrow tunnel and the jaguar comes after me. "**I'm stuck!**" he roars. "That was the plan," I say.

"I need you to let my friends and family go," I tell him.

"After they tried to take my treasure?" he asks.

I nod. "We don't want a single piece of your treasure.

We just want our families back."

The jaguar agrees to let them go,
so I ask Amber and Jun to help me get
him out of the tunnel. Then we find a rope
and help our families climb out of the pit.

Just as we're leaving the cave,
the guards Wu-Chang sent get there.
"You're too late," Amber says proudly.
Emperor Quon laughs. "Yes, the princesses already rescued us!"

Our dads didn't think we could do it, but they are so proud. And that night, there's a beautiful firework display – in honour of the three

bravest
rescuers
in the
land!

The End